MICK McMENACE

Ghost Detective

My name is Mick McMenace.

I'm a ghost.

I'm also a detective.

That makes me a ghost detective – about the only one around.

Here are some of the weird and spooky cases I was asked to solve recently. Can you solve them before I do?

Kaye Umansky was born in Plymouth, Devon. Her favourite books as a child were the *Just William* books, *Alice's Adventures in Wonderland*, *The Hobbit* and *The Swish of the Curtain*. She went to teacher training college, and then she taught in London primary schools for twelve years, specializing in music and drama. In her spare time she sang and played keyboards with a semi-professional soul band.

She now writes full time – or as full time as she can in between trips to Sainsbury's and looking after her husband (Mo), daughter (Ella) and cats (Charlie and Alfie).

Books by Kaye Umansky

PONGWIFFY
PONGWIFFY AND THE GOBLINS' REVENGE
PONGWIFFY AND THE SPELL OF THE YEAR
PONGWIFFY AND THE HOLIDAY OF DOOM
PONGWIFFY AND THE PANTOMIME
PONGWIFFY AND THE SPELLOVISION SONG CONTEST

WILMA'S WICKED REVENGE
WILMA'S WICKED SPELL

THE FWOG PWINCE: THE TWUTH!

PRINCE DANDYPANTS AND THE MASKED AVENGER

For younger readers

THE DRESSED-UP GIANT
GOBLINZ!

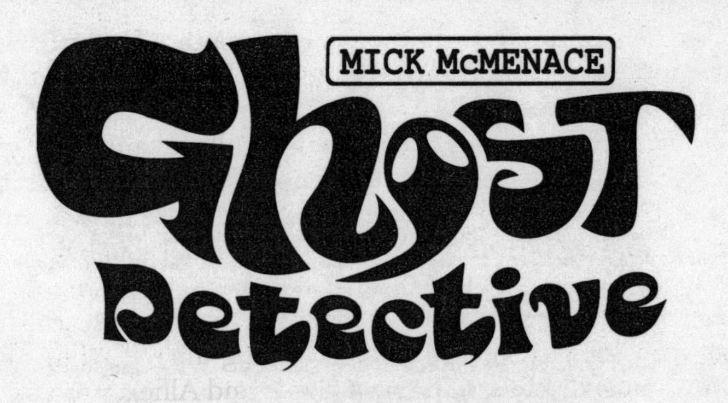

KAYE UMANSKY

Illustrated by Ian Cunliffe

PUFFIN BOOKS

Published by the Penguin Group
Penguin Books Ltd, 80 Strand, London WC2R 0RL, England
Penguin Putnam Inc., 375 Hudson Street, New York, New York 10014, USA
Penguin Books Australia Ltd, 250 Camberwell Road, Camberwell, Victoria 3124, Australia
Penguin Books Canada Ltd, 10 Alcorn Avenue, Toronto, Ontario, Canada M4V 3B2
Penguin Books India (P) Ltd, 11 Community Centre, Panchsheel Park,
New Delhi – 110 017, India
Penguin Books (NZ) Ltd, Cnr Rosedale and Airborne Roads, Albany, Auckland, New Zealand
Penguin Books (South Africa) (Pty) Ltd, 24 Sturdee Avenue, Rosebank 2196, South Africa

Penguin Books Ltd, Registered Offices: 80 Strand, London WC2R 0RL, England

www.penguin.com

First published 2003
1

Set in Baskervill MT

Made and printed in England by Clays Ltd, St Ives plc

British Library Cataloguing in Publication Data
A CIP catalogue record for this book is available from the British Library

ISBN 0-141-31525-3

CONTENTS

CASE 1
THE MYSTERIOUS CASE OF THE DISAPPEARING HEAD

It was 1 a.m. I was in the office. You can find me there most nights. Night-time is when things hot up in down-town Spooksville.

Besides, I'm a ghost. I don't need sleep.

What I *do* need, though, is dough. Yes, folks, I was stony broke. Work had been thin on the ground lately and I was beginning to wonder if I'd ever get another case.

Luckily, the telephone rang.

'McMenace here,' I drawled. That's me. Mick McMenace, Ghost Detective. Weird And Spooky Happenings A Speciality.

'Mr McMenace?' quavered a voice. 'Thank goodness you're there. This is Miss Misty, the Deputy at the Ghoul School. I'm terribly worried. The Head's head's gone missing.'

'Huh? How many heads did you say?'

'Just the one. The Head's.'

'Pity. Two heads are better than one, heh, heh. Just kidding, babe. OK, I'll materialize right on over.'

I set my hat at a stylish angle and

reached for my shades. I'm kinda particular about my appearance. Then I vanished.

Hey, I'm a ghost. It's easy.

I reappeared in the school corridor, looking pretty cool, though I say it myself.

Miss Misty was a disappointment. I wished I hadn't called her 'babe' now. She was one of those drab, faded types, all got up in one of those old-fashioned Victorian outfits. She was dabbing at her eyes with a lace hanky. I could see she was upset. She kept going fuzzy around the edges.

'OK, lady,' I said. 'What's the story?'

'It's Mr Dread, our Headmaster. I went to powder my nose, and when I came back, *this* is how I found him!'

She opened a door and pointed a trembling finger. Behind the desk, drumming his fingers irritably, sat a body in a long, black gown.

Just the body. Above the neck, thin air.

Apart from the missing head, Dread's body seemed in perfect working order. As I stood there staring, he began wildly waving his arms around. Then, suddenly, he shot to his feet

and tripped over the waste-paper basket.

'He can't see where he's going, poor man,' wept Miss Misty, as we helped him into the chair again. 'I keep telling him not to move, but he can't hear me, not without his ears. Oh, what shall we do? Mr Dread is such a harmless man.'

''*Arm*less? I thought he was *head*less,' I joked. I was trying to cheer her up, but she cried even harder. 'OK, lady, calm down. Tell me. Is Dread the kinda guy who loses his head easily?'

'Oh, no. He's very careful. He usually carries it under his arm. Sometimes he puts it on the desk. He's very attached to it. Well, he isn't at the minute, but you know what I mean. He had its eyes tested the other day. Look! Here are his glasses. He can't see a thing without them. He won't be able to write the end-of-term reports. Oh, poor, poor Mr Dread!'

She ran over to stroke his hand. Dread pushed her away, turned his back on us and folded his arms. Obviously sulking.

I picked up the glasses and examined them. They were huge, thick ones. Some ghosts really like to make spectacles of themselves.

'Whoever would steal a head that doesn't belong to them?' cried Miss Misty.

'Somebody who wants to get ahead, I guess,' I wisecracked. I'm always cracking jokes. You need to keep your spirits up in my business. 'But, seriously. If you wanna help your boss, I need answers to a few questions. Who comes in here?'

'Everyone. It's an ever-open door. The staff, pupils, parents, all trooping in and out, always complaining, always late for appointments . . .'

'Hold it. What staff?'

'Well, there's Miss Banshee, she does wailing with the infants. And Frank Enstein, he takes science with class six. Then there's old Mrs Jinx, she teaches

chain rattling. Mr Moonmad, he takes the advanced werewolves. Miss Stickler takes class five for walking through walls . . .'

'Is that it?'

'Well, yes. Except for Zack Zombie, the scaretaker.'

'Bring 'em all in. I feel kinda grumpy. I'll give 'em a cross-examination. Geddit? *Cross-examination* . . .'

Miss Misty wasn't listening. She collared a little werewolf and asked him to take a message. He told her it was play-time and tried to bite her hand. Nasty little nipper.

Eventually, the staff began to drift in, clutching mugs of tea and piles of exercise books. Old Mrs Jinx had her knitting. I don't know what it was, but whatever was going to wear it had six legs.

They were a ghastly-looking bunch. Typical teachers. They started off moaning about missing their break, but soon shut up when they saw their boss slumped forlornly in his chair. If ever a body looked depressed, that one did.

Miss Misty patted his shoulder and tried pouring tea down his neck. He choked. Everybody sniggered, even Miss Misty. It was a real funny choke. (Geddit?)

The last to arrive was Zack Zombie. I had a hunch about him. He had one

too, on his shoulder. Typical scaretaker. Big, mean, spike in one hand and sack full of confiscated footballs in the other.

'Is dis gonna take long?' he growled. 'Cos I got work to do.' He leered and brandished his spike. 'Gotta puncture all dese footballs. Little so-and-sos keep kickin' 'em up in the gutter. Mind if I smoke?'

He reached into his pocket and took out a disgusting old pipe.

'Pipe down, Zombie!' I snapped. He snarled and put it away again.

'There's been a robbery,' I went on. 'Your head's boss has gone missing. I mean your boss's head. Know anything about it?'

'No. Why should I?'

'What about the rest of you?' I asked.

'Well, I'm sure *I* don't know anything,' twittered sweet little Miss Banshee. 'I've been taking wail practice all morning.'

I gave her a reassuring wink. She

didn't do it. Some you just know.

'I was in the lab with class six, harnessing lightning,' chipped in Enstein, the science guy.

I believed him. He had a big bolt in his neck. (Lightning. Bolt. Geddit?)

Old Mrs Jinx looked up from her knitting.

'Nothing to do with me, dearie,' she croaked. 'I'm part-time.'

Too doddery. She'd trip over her knitting.

'Or me,' growled Mr Moonmad. 'I feel highly insulted by the suggestion.'

Hmm. Maybe.

'Me too,' snapped Miss Stickler, fixing me with a laser glare. 'What gives you the right to accuse any of us? We're teachers, not head hunters. We educate, not decapitate. This is an outrage!'

She was furious. I half expected her to give me a hundred lines and make me go and sit in the corner. If *she'd* taken the Head's head, I didn't want to be the one to say so.

'The fact remains,' I said sternly, 'that Dread's head's gone walkies, and I'm here to find the culprit.'

'Are you a policeman, then?'

'No,' said Miss Misty, before I could reply. 'I didn't think we'd want to involve the police at this stage. Mr McMenace is a private eye.'

'Aye?' growled Zack Zombie, staring at me.

'*Eye*,' I corrected him. Some people just can't spell.

'What I want to know is, who'll write the Head's comments on the end-of-term reports?' asked little Miss Banshee.

'Not me!' chorused the rest of the staff hastily.

'I will,' said Miss Misty briskly.

Everyone's mouth dropped open in shock.

'It's the least I can do,' she added, putting away her hanky. 'We can't disappoint the parents. I'll take assembly too. And I'll telephone the chief in-spectre and break the sad news. And I'll do dinner duty. After all, I'm Acting Head now.'

Just then, a bell rang. Everyone's shoulders slumped.

'Oh, well,' sighed Enstein. 'Break's over. Back to class.'

They all produced red pens and began to troop out with their empty mugs.

'Hold it!' I said sharply. 'Not so fast. Just come back in here, boys and girls. This may amaze you, but I've figured out who did this dirty deed.'

Can you?

Here is Mick's solution

Miss Misty did it. All that crying was put on. She wanted Dread's job. I guessed the shocking truth the minute she volunteered to do all the extra work. What teacher would offer to take that on, unless there was something in it for them?

All became clear when I ordered Zack Zombie to empty his sack of footballs on to the carpet. Sure enough, there was Dread's head, hair all mussed up, eyes rolling pathetically and mouth stuck firmly shut with school sticky-tape.

When we gave it back to the body and removed the tape so that the poor guy could talk, everything became clear. Miss Misty had picked her moment carefully. She had waited until Dread

put his head on the desk and removed his glasses. He can't see without them, remember? Then she picked up the head, sticky-taped the mouth and sneaked off to Zombie's hut, where she buried it in the bag of soon-to-be-punctured footballs before coming back to raise the alarm. She was fed up with being the Deputy and doing all the work, she said.

I dunno. Teachers. They're in a class of their own.

CASE 2
THE COMPLICATED CASE OF THE KIDNAPPED CAT

It was 1 a.m. I was hunched over a cup of coffee at Louie's Diner, reading the *Spooksville Gazette*. The headlines screamed:

Major Crackdown!
New Police Chief Wages War On Crime!

I was the only customer. Everyone

else had homes to go to. All I had was a desk, a phone and a filing cabinet. Yes, folks. I was so broke I was camping in the office. Only one light works, the roof leaks and it's real small, so it was a one-lamp, damp, cramped camp, heh, heh.

I dunno why I'm laughing. It was horrible.

'More coffee, Mr McMenace?' said Big Louie, coming over with the pot. He's not the brightest zombie in the world, but he's a good sort.

'Sure, Louie,' I sighed. 'Why not?'

'Because it tastes awful,' said Big Louie, after careful thought.

'I'll have it anyway,' I said. 'Nothing better to do.'

'Business bad again, huh?' tutted Big Louie sympathetically, pouring coffee

into my lap. Did I mention he's cross-eyed? Luckily, it was cold and so weak it didn't even stain my trousers.

'You can say that again,' I said.

'OK,' said Big Louie. 'Business bad again, huh?'

'Yeah,' I said. Well, it was. Like the paper said, Spooksville had a new police chief in-spectre. His name was Major Crackdown and he was ex-army, and very thorough. Since his appointment, the town had become a crime-free zone. No burglaries. No bank raids. No mysterious dames knocking at my door, begging me to find their missing diamonds. Nobody needed my services. Times were kinda hard.

Luckily, the phone rang.

Unluckily, it wasn't for me.

'Someone from de Cat of de Year Show remindin' me to fill in an entry form,' said Big Louie. 'If you don't mind, I'm just nipping in de back to feed Ben Her. I t'ink her De Luxe Chickenballs are at room temperature.'

'Sure, Louie,' I said. You wouldn't

think a big zombie like him would be such an old softie about a cat, but where Ben Her is concerned, Louie is putty. She's one of those fat, snooty, cream-coloured, fluffy types. Big Louie puts her in for cat shows. She wins paws down every time. He slaves all day over a hot stove, cooking fancy treats that she never eats, preferring to dine in the bins up the alley. He even wrote a poem about her once. He showed it to me, all proud. It went:

ODE TO MY
LUVLY CAT
Benny Herry's
Soft and purry.
Oh, I forgot.
And furry.

(She was just plain Ben before she had kittens, in case you're wondering.)

I sat there, sipping Louie's awful coffee. Out back, I could hear him calling for Ben Her.

'Benny, Benny, Benny! Her, Her, Her! Come on, sweetie, dinner's ready. Daddy's blown on it – it's nice and cool. Dat's funny. Where's she gone? Come to daddy, angel. Bennybennybenny-benny ...'

I reached for my hat, tossed a note on the counter and went out into the night. (The note said: *IOU six bucks.*)

Louie's is in the shady part of town. As I cut through the alley, just up ahead of me, I thought I heard a cat. Either that, or a very clever dog.

'*Miaaaaaaaaoooooooooooooow!*' it went,

followed by a lot of angry spitting.

Just as I reached the street, a long, low limousine pulled away from the kerb and purred off into the night. The windows were dark. The number plate was painted out.

Funny. Oh, well. None of my business.

I gave a shrug, went back to the office and slept like a baby (i.e. waved my legs about and howled so loud I woke the whole neighbourhood, heh, heh. Just kidding).

The next day, I materialized in at Louie's for my morning doughnut. I could only afford one a week. I was going in and taking a small bite every day. Big Louie kept it under a dish for me, away from the flies.

I found him all worried, writing out posters for a missing cat.

MISSIN, it read. **BEN HER. SHEEZ GOT A CREEM COAT AND WISKERS. IF FOWND, PLEEZ BRING BAK TO LOUIE. REWARD.**

'You'd best explain she's a cat,' I told Louie. 'My gran has got a cream coat and whiskers.'

'Good point, Mr McMenace,' said Louie, and began adding **SHEEZ A CAT** to the bottom of the posters.

'I'll help you stick 'em up, Louie,' I

offered. Well, I felt sorry for him.

'Gee, thanks, Mr McMenace. I don't want to go out in case she comes home.'

So that was how I came to be sticking up Missing Cat posters all over Spooksville.

They attracted quite a bit of interest.

A banshee came up and looked over my shoulder, then hurried quickly away. But not before I noticed she had a long, fresh scratch down one cheek.

A little old lady staggered by, laden down with milk, flea spray and what smelled like fish heads. I asked her what they were for. She told me they were for her pet canary, then scuttled off, cackling. Some canary.

A farmer drove by on a donkey cart.

'Fine day,' I said, seeing him peering darkly from beneath his straw hat.

'Ar,' he mumbled. 'Well, I can't stay 'ere chattin'. Rats in the barn. Shame I ain't got a cat.' And he drove off, giving me crafty looks over his shoulder.

I didn't see anybody suspicious, though.

I had just finished putting up the last poster when I felt a hand on my shoulder.

'Come with me, sir, if you please,' said a polite voice. I turned around and found myself staring into a navy-blue chest. It wasn't a pol*ite* voice. It was a pol*ice* voice. What a difference one little letter makes.

'What's the problem?' I asked. 'I'm just helping a friend out.'

'Why? Is he in?'

'Very funny,' I said grimly. 'Look, don't you know there's a cat burglar out there? Why waste time with me?'

'It'll all be made clear back at the station, sir,' said the cop. And to my amazement, he took out a pair of handcuffs and cuffed me.

Wisely, I didn't cuff him back.

Major Crackdown's hard eyes bored into me from behind the desk. He had wire glasses and steel-rimmed hair (or perhaps it was the other way around).

My keen eye flickered about his office. A large, framed photo of Crackdown holding a huge, fluffy moggy stood on his desk. On the wall was a certificate proclaiming that some creature called Tinkyboo had been awarded second prize at a pet show. Obviously an animal lover. But I can't say I liked him. Oh, he was a hot

shot all right. But something about him smelled fishy.

'So what's the story, Chief?' I drawled.

'We're arresting you, McMenace. End of story.'

Casually, I reached forward and plucked lightly at his jacket.

'Just a stray hair,' I explained, leaning back and cleverly pocketing his wallet. I didn't like this guy. I wanted his address so that I could send him hate mail. 'So,' I went on, 'you're arresting me. What's the charge?'

'Bill posting. It's an offence to stick up posters in this town, as I think you well know.'

'Better than sticking up the bank,' I wisecracked. 'Anyway, like I said, I was only doing a friend a favour.'

'The fact remains that you broke the law. I've heard about you, McMenace. You're a troublemaker. I'm holding you in the cell until your case comes up.'

'*Whaaaaat?*' I gasped. 'You can't do that!'

He could, though.

Ten minutes later, the cell door clanged shut and footsteps walked away, leaving me alone in pitch darkness.

Now, I know what you're thinking. You're thinking, he's a ghost. Why can't he just escape through the wall?

I'll tell you why. In Spooksville, the police cell walls are coated with ghost-resistant paint. How else are they gonna keep the criminals in? I found this out painfully, when I tried walking through one.

Moaning loudly, I felt my way to a bench and collapsed, clutching my sore head.

Suddenly, to my surprise, there came a scraping noise and a match flared. I found myself gazing at a skinny old man lying on a low bed with long, wild, grey hair. (The hair was on the old man. Not the bed.)

His whiskery face grinned at me in the light of a candle.

'Tee, hee, hee,' he giggled. 'Tee, hee, hee!'

'No thanks,

gramps,' I said. 'I prefer coffee.' (Geddit?)

'See you tried walkin' through the wall,' he cried in a thin, high voice. 'They all tries that, tee, hee. I keep tellin' 'em it won't work. I knows these things. I been here years. I'm an old lag.'

'Yeah? What do they call you, gramps?'

'Old Lagg. I'm in for speedin'. Me brakes were bad and I wanted to get 'ome quick before I 'ad an accident. So 'ere I sits, all alone in the dark, livin' on bread and water.'

'Tough,' I sympathized.

'No, it ain't,' said Old Lagg cheerfully. 'I quite likes bread and water. And nobody can see me, so I don't 'ave to wash.'

'Well, it sounds pretty bad to me.'

'Yeah. Well, sometimes I gets a bit stir crazy. Then I goes out to stretch me legs. They're getting quite long now, see?' He pointed down at his skinny old legs, which were indeed quite long. 'I was five foot three when I came in. Now I'm six foot two.'

'Hold it,' I said. 'Did you just say *go out*?'

'Oh, yeah. Through the secret tunnel.'

'There's a *tunnel*?'

'Yeah. Didn't I mention it? It's me life's work. I dug it meself, using a plastic fork. I comes and goes as I pleases. I'll show you!'

He leapt to his feet and began pushing his bed to one side. My trained eye noticed something odd about it.

'Have you sawn the legs off that bed?' I enquired.

'Yep. I needed to lie low for a bit, tee, hee. Here's the tunnel.'

To my amazement, I found myself staring down into a large hole.

'Where did you hide all the soil?' I asked curiously.

'Mixed it in with the water and drank it,' explained Old Lagg. 'And the crunchy bits I ate with the bread. A bit like peanut butter.'

I admit I was impressed. The man must have been eating gravel for years. I bet his stomach felt rocky.

'Well,' I said. 'I gotta go. I'm working on a case. You coming?'

'No,' said Old Lagg. 'They'll be bringing supper down soon. Can I 'ave your bread and water?'

Minutes later, I was wriggling through the tunnel. It was a tight fit. My shoulders were wider than Old Lagg's. Luckily, there wasn't far to go. I felt a welcome breeze on my face, and suddenly my head popped out into the cool night air.

The tunnel ended behind a bush in the police station car park. I heaved myself up and out and was just brushing mud from my hat when I found myself caught in the crossbeams of headlights.

A car door slammed, official-sounding feet approached and a weary voice said, 'Going somewhere, sir?'

It was the cop who had arrested me the first time.

'Listen, officer,' I said, trying to be reasonable. 'This is crazy. I'm being held on some trumped-up charge to keep me off the cat case. Did I mention I'm looking for a stolen cat?'

'Yes, sir. You told me that already.'

'Ah,' I said. 'But what I *didn't* tell you is that, incredible though it may seem, I've worked out who the culprit is.'

Yes, folks. Gasp if you like. Once again, my powers of deduction had come to my aid. I knew who had dunnit!

Do you?

Here is Mick's solution

Major Crackdown did it. After some persuasion, the cop finally agreed to drive me to the chief in-spectre's house. When we got there, we found him relaxing in his study with a truckload of prize cats on his lap. They all looked like Ben Her.

Clearly, the guy was cat crazy. Apparently, he entered them for competitions as a hobby, but Big Louie's Ben Her beat them every time. That's why he stole her. He had removed the name tag from her collar. His evil plan was to pass her off as his own.

How did I know this? Well, there was the photo on his desk, of course, and the certificate for second prize displayed on the wall. And remember I said I smelled something fishy about him? It was his hands. He had clearly been cooking up fish heads for his beloved pets. But what finally convinced me was the cream cat hair I removed from his jacket when I stole his wallet!

He resigned the next day. Crime in Spooksville immediately went up, which was good news for me.

All the cats at Crackdown's pad looked the same – fat, cream-coloured and snooty. So how did Big Louie tell which one was his? Easy. He put down dishes of lovingly prepared Prawncheeks à la Posh. These proved highly popular. Only one cat turned her nose up and refused to eat them. Ben Her, of course. So now they're back together again and Louie's happy.

He gave me a reward. Unlimited coffee forever.

Hmm.

CASE 3
THE TERRIFYING CASE OF THE TARTAN TROUSERS

It was 1 a.m. I was in my office, playing Twister. I was having a knotty problem involving my left ear and my right foot.

Luckily, the telephone rang.

I sorted myself out pronto and snatched it up. It was the phone company telling me they were cutting me off because I hadn't paid the bill. I slammed it down and put my head in my hands. Yes, folks, I was broke again. I needed some dough, and quickly.

Just then, to my amazement, there was a tap on my office door. Funny. I thought it was usually on the sink, heh, heh. (Tap. Sink. Geddit?)

Seriously, though, I like clients who knock. It shows respect. Most just barge on in through the wall.

'Come in,' I called. 'The door's open.'

I smelled her perfume before I saw her. Some sort of flower. Roses, perhaps. Or violets? Or maybe cauliflower.

'Are you the private detective?' she said, a bit nervously.

'That's me, honey. Take a seat. But

leave me the desk, I might need it, heh, heh.'

She sank gratefully into a chair. She was a good-looking dame. She had sparkling blue eyes and bright-red fingernails. Or was it was the other way around? Her hair was green, but I kinda liked it.

'I can't stay long,' she said. 'I'm on my way to work.'

I wondered what kind of job she did that required a glittery evening gown and painful shoes. She told me her name was Gloria Glamorre and (much to my surprise) that she was the singer at Louie's. Apparently, he's smartened up his act and washed the tablecloths and put red paper over the light bulbs. He's hired Gloria and is calling it a club. I hadn't been there for weeks. I couldn't take any more of his coffee.

'So what's the story, lady?' I asked. 'My guess is you're not here to sing.'

'No,' she said. 'I'm not. I've got a big problem, Mr McMenace.'

'Call me Mick. What's the problem, Miss Glamorre?'

'I'm being stalked. *By a pair of tartan trousers!*'

'Uh-huh,' I said, reaching for a pad and pencil. This sounded routine. Trouser hauntings are ten a penny in Spooksville. Not tartan ones, mind.

'Wherever I go, I see them,' said Gloria Glamorre with a shiver. 'They hide behind the aisles in the spooker-market. They sit behind me on buses. They come to hear me sing at Louie's. Then they follow me home. Last night, I woke up to find them doing the Highland fling in my bedroom! I was absolutely terrified.'

'I'll bet,' I tutted. This was shabby behaviour, for trousers.

'When I screamed, they jumped out the window and ran off.'

‘What kind of tartan?’ I asked, busily making notes.

‘Sort of red,’ she said vaguely. ‘And green. With a hole in the knee. Horrible shape.’

‘Never a kilt?’

‘No. Trousers.’

‘And they never say anything?’

‘No. What would they say?’

She had a point.

‘But they haven’t actually done anything,’ I pointed out. ‘There’s no law against trousers. They haven’t attacked you, have they?’

‘They might. How do you know what they’ll do? The other week, I was having a picnic and they folded themselves on a park bench, then leapt up and ran off with my pudding.’

'Which was?'

'A trifle.'

'I guess you were a trifle fed up.'

'I sure was.'

'So what do you want me to do?'

'Well – stop them. I can pay, if that's what you're worried about. Louie's not exactly generous, but it's more than I got when I was working night shifts in the bakery.'

'Robinson Crusoe did a forty-hour week and still had all the work done by Friday,' I wisecracked.

She smiled. I was liking her more and more.

'OK, Miss Glamorre.' I sat back in my chair. 'I've got all the details I need. I must say, the case interests me. It's not really a whodunnit. It's more a whytheydoinit. These trousers hang around Louie's, you say?'

'Every night. They sit on a stool at the bar and cross their legs at me. Once, they held up a sign. It said: *You're Rubbish, You Are.* It's very off-putting. Anyway, I must go. I'm on soon. What are you doing?'

'I'm coming with you,' I said grimly, reaching for my hat and shades. 'I need to see these trousers in action.'

Big Louie was pleased to see me. He had swapped his greasy apron for a suit and wore a badge reading: *Club Manager.*

'Hey, Mr McMenace,' he greeted

me, all smiles, when I materialized at the bar. 'Long time no see. Coffee?'

'No thanks, Louie,' I said.

He poured it in my lap anyway.

'So what do you t'ink of de place?' he asked proudly. Adding, 'I'm a club now.'

I looked around. In the dim, red light, I could see the tables were packed. A small stage had been set up in one corner. A spook with a saxophone was putting up a mike stand. Another was tuning his guitar. A third was bashing on his drum kit, in that annoying way that drummers do.

There was no sign of Gloria. I'd arrived after her, because I stopped off at the dry cleaner's on the way. I'd got a copy of the *Spooksville Gazette* too, while I was at it.

'You've done a great job, Louie,' I said. 'I like the lights.'

'Yeah. I put red paper on dem. I got a singer too. She's really packin' 'em in. Dis is de town hot spot now.'

'Glad to hear it. How's Ben Her?'

'Still a winner, Mr McMenace, t'anks to you.'

'Say, Louie. Got a couple of questions for you.'

'Anyt'ing, Mr McMenace.'

'Does a pair of tartan trousers come in here? Sit at the bar? Act suspicious?'

Just then, there came a drum roll. It was followed by a sausage roll. Then an egg salad one, which came whizzing over my shoulder, sprinkling me with sliced tomato. The crowd was getting restless.

'Where's Gloria?' shouted a table of vampires.

'Yeah!' agreed a reedy voice, which I recognized. Old Lagg was out of jail again. 'We want Gloria!'

The crowd took up the chant. A spotlight came on – and there she was, in her glittery gown. She opened her mouth and began to sing.

She was good. I don't know about show business.

I've never been on stage, although I had my leg in a cast once, heh, heh. But Gloria was the tops. I particularly enjoyed her version of 'I Will Survive'. In fact, I was so taken with it I almost didn't notice the pair of tartan trousers sitting on the stool next to me.

Big Louie and his coffee pot had moved away. I looked at the trousers. The trousers looked at me. At least, I think they did. I'm not an expert on these things. Who knows how trousers operate? Anyway, the knees were facing my way. I was just about to challenge them when Gloria's act came to an end. She bowed, waved and vanished.

'Encore!' shouted the crowd. 'More! More!'

But she didn't reappear. I guess Louie doesn't pay her enough for encores.

I turned back to the trousers. They had gone. Where they had sat, there was an empty stool. Grimly, I picked up my paper and the bag of stuff from the dry cleaner's and followed.

Gloria was walking down the empty street. I heard her high heels clacking ahead of me in the distance. A short way behind her were the tartan trousers, ducking in and out of the doorways. And behind *them* was me. I wanted to follow and see what they would do. I was curious to know the motive behind all this.

At one point, the trousers stopped and turned round in the road. I had a feeling they realized they were being followed. I knew what to do, of course. Pretend to be an innocent bystander waiting for a bus. Good thinking, eh?

I casually leaned against a lamp post and opened the *Gazette*. The headlines read:

Exclusive! Spooksville Empire Closing Down!

I glanced at the first paragraph. Sure enough, it was curtains for the old theatre. Seemed like it had been playing to empty houses for some time. Shows had been cancelled due to lack of interest and a lot of the old acts were out of work. Mind you, they were terrible anyway. I know. My mum used to take me there when I was a kid.

Uncle Ghoul and His Furry Friends. The Juggling Witches. Corny stuff like that.

So. Nobody wanted to be entertained any more. Mind you, Big Louie was doing OK.

Hmm. Interesting. I read on.

A short while later, when I'd finished the piece, I looked up. The trousers had fallen for the innocent-bystander scam. They were moving off again, about to vanish round the corner. I folded the paper and hurried on.

Gloria had reached her place – a tall, thin house opening directly on to the street. She was standing at the door, fumbling for her key, when something really strange happened.

The trousers that had been stalking

her suddenly stopped skulking in the shadows and stood up straight. They had a distinct air of menace. At the same time, *another almost identical pair emerged from a side alley*! Another pair with a patch on the backside suddenly loomed up from behind a dustbin. Two

more pairs jumped out from behind a lamp post and yet another came sneaking out from a dark doorway. Six pairs in all! A troupe of tartan trousers. All cut really narrow and tapering at the ankle, just the way I don't like them.

Gloria turned, and went deathly pale. The trousers were closing in. She tried to make a run for it, but the nearest pair stuck out a leg and tripped her up. She fell to the ground with a

sharp scream. The poor girl was terrified. I had to do something, and quick.

'Hold it right there!' I commanded, stepping forward. 'Leave the lady alone! I know who you are and why you're doing this!'

Yeah. You heard. I'd only gone and done it again.

So. Do you know the answer?

Here is Mick's solution

The Tartan Trousers were a dancing troupe from up north. They had been around for years, trading on their quaint appeal, but, recently, audiences had been dwindling. Nobody came to their shows any more. Well, they were tartan. They just weren't fashionable.

So, in desperation, they had pooled the contents of their pockets and come to Spooksville, hoping for one more stab at fame.

At first, things looked promising. They got a week's trial booking at the Spooksville Empire, but ticket sales were so poor that all their shows were cancelled. Why? Because Gloria was singing at Louie's, that's why. Who'd go and watch boring old tartan trousers do some tired dance routine when they could listen to Gloria? The trousers knew they weren't a patch on her. So they hatched a cunning plan to scare Gloria off. If she gave up singing and went back to the bakery, they would have the town's entertainment sewn up.

'So there you have it,' I finished. 'A simple case of trouser jealousy.' I was pleased to note that Gloria was speechless with admiration. I pointed sternly to the trousers. 'You should all be ashamed of yourselves. Line up to take your punishment.'

The trousers drooped. My speech had left them thoroughly crumpled.

Meaningfully, I picked up the bag from the dry cleaner's and took out a handful of wire hangers. Sadly, they shuffled into a line. They knew what was coming.

You know what happens to worn-out trousers. They get hung up neatly and put away for life. Cruel, maybe, but when you're past it, you're past it. Anyway, that's just what I did. Rest assured, those troublesome trousers won't be let out for a very long time – if ever.

How had I worked this out? Simple. I read it in the paper. I didn't tell Gloria that, though.

CASE 4
THE CURIOUS CASE OF THE STOLEN CHRISTMAS PUDDING RECIPE

It was 1 a.m. It was also Christmas Eve and snowing. I stared gloomily out of my office window, eating bread and sipping water because I was broke. What's new?

Outside, the dark streets of Spooksville were rapidly emptying. Two empty suits of armour were by the pillar box, posting some last-minute chain mail. (Armour. Chain mail. Oh, never mind.)

Headless coachmen were crashing into each other in their haste to get back to the staff party. A couple of vampires walked by carrying a Christmas tree. Happy families of mummies, deadies and little spooks headed home for supper, chattering about the phantomime they'd just seen. *Ghouldilocks*, I think it was.

And me? All I had was the choice of tinned spookhetti or warmed-up ghoulash. If it wasn't for my Wraithways Individual Christmas Pudding Portion, I wouldn't have known it was Christmas. (I always shop at Wraithways because their Sad 'n' Lonely range does single portions. They taste awful, but they're cheap.)

Usually, I'm an upbeat, wisecracking kinda guy, but that night I was so low my chin was sinking through the table. I almost ate the Pudding Portion then and there, leaving myself nothing to look forward to on Christmas Day.

Luckily, the telephone rang.

'Is that the McMenace Detective Agency?' The voice sounded slimy.

'Sure is,' I drawled. 'McMenace speaking. How can I help?'

'This is Slimy, sir, Lord Humphrey Howling's butler. I'm ringing from Howling Hall.'

Humphrey Howling, huh? I'd heard of him. If you're talking big bucks, Howling's the ghost with the most. The guy was loaded. I'd seen pictures of him in *Vague,* the society magazine. One of those la-di-da seventeenth-century wig-and-silk-trouser types. Lives in a mansion in the country.

Rumour had it he owed his vast fortune to the success of Howling's, a swanky uptown eating joint, famed for its Christmas pudding. They say the secret recipe has been passed down for centuries. It's so good, people eat it all year round, even in high summer.

Not me. The prices are too fancy for my pocket.

But Slimy was still talking.

'I'm afraid a dastardly robbery has been committed, sir. Someone has stolen the famous Howling Christmas Pudding Recipe from His Lordship's safe. Ah, 'tis a sad, sad day.'

A stolen pudding recipe? This was stirring stuff. (Geddit?)

'OK, Slimy, don't panic. Tell your master I'll materialize right on over.'

'Oh, thank you, sir. His Lordship will meet you at the scene of the crime. By the safe in the library in, shall we say, half a minute?'

'Make it thirty seconds, heh, heh,' I wisecracked. I was cheering up. This sounded interesting.

I tipped my hat, put on my shades, then transported myself to Howling Hall. The beauty of being a ghost is you don't have to rely on the buses.

I didn't mean to appear in the ballroom. I had aimed for the library, but the snow had caused freak atmospheric conditions. It happens.

There was a party in progress. I showed up right in the middle of the dance floor, directly in the path of Henry VIII and Shakespeare, who

waltzed straight through me with no apology. All three of us were ghosts, so it didn't hurt, but I found it kinda irritating. Manners cost nothing, right?

My keen eye flicked around, giving the place the once-over. My other eye wasn't so keen and just stared straight ahead, heh, heh.

It was the usual crowd. Royalty, mainly, with a few hangers on. Queen Victoria was there. Catch her missing a party. So was Queen Elizabeth, surrounded by the usual Sir Francis Drake lookalikes. A group of drowned seamen were waving seaweed around and doing a hippy dance in a circle. They tried to get me to join in. I told them I didn't move in that sort of circle. (Geddit?)

Joan of Arc was there, eating a sausage roll and talking tactics with Napoleon. The entire ghostly crew of the *Flying Dutchman* was playing cards. An old guy in rags was dragging his ball and chain through the dancers, rattling a tin that read: *Under Curse, Please Give Generously.*

Some creep from the *Spooksville Gazette* suddenly bobbed up in front of me, waving a camera and demanding an interview. He wore a badge marked *PRESS*. So I did, and my finger went right through him. It was a joke, but he didn't see the funny side. The funny side was his back, where my finger poked out.

Just then, I saw Joan clanking towards me, waving her sword. There's something about dames in armour. Hastily, I faded out and made for the library.

This time, I got it right. I appeared directly behind Lord Howling, who was on his knees next to the open safe, weeping into a lace hanky. These courtly types are pathetic.

'OK, buster, what's the story?' I always say that. I think it sounds really good.

Howling scrambled to his feet and stamped his foot.

'Isn't it obvious? I have been wobbed! Don't just hover there. Do something!'

I'm a plain-speaking guy, but if there's one thing I can't stand, it's rudeness.

'Listen, pal,' I said. 'I'm the detective. We do things my way, right? First, my fee. I don't want your dough. I want unlimited amounts of free pudding at Howling's forever. With a table at the window. Plus expenses.'

'I'm not sure we want your sort in Howling's,' sniffed His Lordship, all hoity-toity. ''Tis vewy exclusive.'

'Take it or leave it.'

'Well, I don't have much choice, do I?'

'Nope. So. What happened?'

'Lawks, how should *I* know? You're the detective – figure it out. Some wotten wobber's sneaked in, opened my safe and stolen my highly secwet Wecipe. Cwistmas Pudding is the most expensive item on Howling's menu. Nobody else can make it, so we charge what we like.'

'Why would anyone go to all that trouble, I wonder?' I pondered. I mean, I like Christmas pudding as much as the next guy, but hey!

'Why do you think? Because they want to open a wival eating house and put me out of business, of course!'

Uh-huh. That made sense.

'Any ideas who?'

'Anyone! Cook, the servants, the guests. They're all jealous. I don't twust any of them. Oh, how can this have happened?'

Howling started howling again. I left him to it.

I floated around the room, looking for clues. I didn't really know what I was hoping to find. Floury fingerprints and a dropped cook's hat? One of Joan's gauntlets, perhaps? Ball-and-chain skid marks on the floor? Seaweed, possibly? A crumpled-up royal decree signed *Henry* in the waste-paper basket? Hairs from the beards of the Francis Drakes? A dropped ace of spades from the crew of the *Flying Dutchman*? A Shakespearean sonnet? Victoria's hanky? Elizabeth's crown? Napoleon's wallet?

Funnily enough, I found all of these. The library was stiff with clues. I couldn't move without tripping over another one. Howling was weeping too hard to notice.

'Tell me more about this Pudding,' I said. 'What's the big deal?'

'Why, 'tis the best in the world! My gweat-gweat-gweat-gwandmamma invented it. She gave stwict instwuctions *never* to let it go out of the family. Even Cook is sworn to secwecy. I have been offered whole kingdoms in exchange for the Wecipe. But I've never been tempted. Do you know why?'

'Because you're an old meanie?'

'No.' His voice sank to a thrilling whisper. ''Tis because of the Curse.'

'The Curse? There's a Curse?' My heart sank. Things were complicated enough without a Curse.

'Of course there's a Curse,' snapped Lord Howling. 'And 'tis a vewy howwible one.'

'What, your legs fall off or something?'

'Worse. Should the Wecipe fall into stwange hands, my luck will change and I shall lose all my money. Oh, bother, *bother*! I shall be forced to sell Howling Hall! I shall be a pauper!'

'Relax,' I said soothingly. 'Look, forget the Curse. There's something fishy about it. I think it's a red herring, heh, heh. Let's stick with the facts. We've got a stolen recipe, a library full of clues and a house full of suspects, any of whom could have done it. Correct?'

'Cowwect.'

The case was turning out to be tricky. That's the trouble with crime solving when everyone involved is a spook. There's no privacy. Anyone can walk through the wall whenever the mood takes them. Not a nice thought when you're in the bathroom.

Just at that moment, a smooth-looking guy in a bow tie floated through the oak panelling. This must be Slimy, the butler.

'Beg pardon, Your Lordship. I took the liberty of rounding up the suspects. I thought Mr McMenace would want to interview them. Shall I show them in one at a time?'

'It's Christmas! Send 'em all in! Let's have a party!' I cried.

Instantly, the library was filled with ghost guests. There were loads, but the advantage of being ghostly is that you can overlap.

'OK, folks,' I said crisply. 'Listen up. There's been a robbery. The Howling Christmas Pudding Recipe's gone missing and you're all suspects. Nobody leaves until they've given a statement.'

There was an angry stir. A couple of ghosts dropped their heads in shock. One of the Francis Drakes fainted. A woman in an apron burst into tears. My quick brain told me that this must be Cook. Why? Because she wore a tall white hat and had a badge saying: *COOK*.

'Oh, Master 'Umphrey, 'ow could you? 'Ow could you suspect poor old Betsy Muffin, 'ose family's cooked for you and yer father and 'is father afore …'

The rest of it was lost in sobs.

'Well, that's *really* nice!' blustered Henry VIII. 'That's charming, I must say! Invite all your friends round, then accuse 'em of theft! That's the last time I come to one of your balls, Humphrey. What's more, I shan't eat at Howling's ever again!'

There was general agreement. Queen Victoria said One had never been so insulted in One's life, and Elizabeth agreed. The Francis Drakes started muttering. The drowned seamen shook their seaweed. The crew of the *Flying Dutchman* threatened mutiny. The old boy rattled his chain. Shakespeare remarked that he didn't even *like* Christmas pudding. Napoleon and Joan both declared war.

At this point, I decided that things

had gone on quite long enough. You see, amazing as this may seem, I had worked it out. Yes, folks. I knew exactly who the thief was!

Well? Whodunnit?

Here is Mick's solution

Slimy did it. He planted all the clues in the library, attempting to frame everybody. But he made a fatal mistake. He forgot to leave a clue for himself! My keen eye spotted that, amongst all the evidence, there was no bow tie. When I ordered him to turn out his pockets, he immediately confessed and sheepishly returned the Recipe to Lord Howling, who sacked him on the spot.

It turned out that he was not Lord Howling's regular butler, whose name was Smoothy and who was visiting his aunt. Also, he was in the pay of Wraithways, which wanted to improve

the quality of its Pudding Portions, and about time too.

Not that I care. These days, I eat at Howling's. Happy Christmas, folks!